USBORNE
Illustrated
Stories
for
Bedtime

USBORNE
Illustrated
Stories
for
Bedtime

Contents

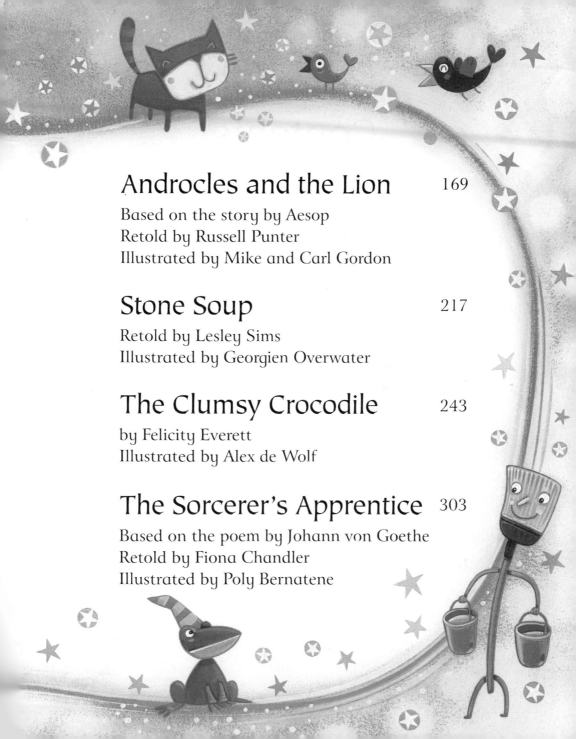

King Donkey Ears

There was once a king with a terrible secret. He was so ashamed of it, he couldn't even share it with his best friend, Sidney.

In fact, the only person
who ever knew was the person
who cut his hair. For, hidden under his
crown, the king had... donkey's ears!

Every month, the king had his hair cut. Each time, a new hairdresser was summoned to the palace and gasped as the king removed his crown.

As soon as his haircut was finished, the king sent the unfortunate hairdresser to jail so his secret didn't get out.

Shh!

In July, it was Meg's turn. She was
rather worried, as she had several friends
who had cut the king's hair and never
been seen again.

Meg was shocked when she saw the king's ears, but she didn't say so.

Oh! What l-lovely hair
Your Majesty has.

Quickly, she took out her comb and scissors and got to work.

Meg was an excellent hairdresser. But as soon as she had finished, the king called for a guard.

Take her to jail!

"Jail?" said Meg. "Didn't you like the haircut? Please don't send me to jail. My mother is sick. She needs me."

The king thought of his own mother. She would be horrified if he sent this poor girl to jail leaving her mother to fend for herself.

He didn't even like putting people in jail, but he had to keep his secret.

"Do you promise that you will never, ever tell a single person about my..." He coughed, "...ears?" he said hurriedly.

I promise!

Meg threw herself at his feet. "I promise! I promise! If only you'll let me go, I won't tell anyone."

That night in bed, Meg could think of only one thing. "The king has donkey's ears! The king has donkey's ears!"

It was such a fantastic, ludicrous, enormous secret, she simply had to share it.

I'm going to burst if I don't tell!

At last, she had an idea. The king had made her promise not to tell a person. So she wouldn't tell a person... she'd tell a tree.

Unable to wait, she ran to the forest in her nightgown and whispered to the trunk of the first tree she reached.

At once, Meg felt better. She had let the secret out but no one would ever know.

A few weeks later, a woodcutter came along. He chopped down several trees – including the tree Meg had whispered to.

This might not have mattered, but the tree was sawn into wood and the wood was sold to a man who made harps.

Soon after that, the king gave a concert. Everyone was eager to hear the star of the show, Helena, play her new harp.

But, as Helena plucked the strings, the strangest song came out, sung in a high, warbly voice.

The king's got donkey's ears...

The king's got donkey's ears...

The king was furious. He leaped from his throne. "You told my secret," he roared at Meg.

The king's best friend came over.
"Do you mean your ears?" said Sidney.
"They're not a secret. We all know."
  "And you don't mind?" asked the king.

"Of course not!" Sidney
declared. "No other kingdom
has a king with such a
remarkable feature."

So the king let all the hairdressers out of jail that very day.

And he learned to love his ears just
as they were.

The Enormous Turnip

Early one morning, a farmer set off, whistling, to his turnip field.

One of the turnips towered above the rest, sticking up out of the ground and sprouting huge green leaves.

"That one must be ready to pull," thought the farmer. "It's gigantic!"

He grabbed hold of the huge green leaves and gave the turnip a tug. Nothing happened.

He tugged some more.

The turnip didn't move.

The farmer's wife saw him puffing and panting.

"That looks hard work,"
she thought. "Hold on dear,"
she called. "I'll come and help.".

She wrapped her arms around her husband and held on tight. The farmer grabbed hold of the leaves once more and took a deep breath.

"One, two, three... **heeeeeeave**!"
he panted. And they both tugged
with all their might.

The turnip didn't move.

Up in the apple tree, Jack saw his
parents puffing and panting.

"Do you
need help?"
he shouted.

Jack jumped down from the apple tree, ran to the turnip field and gripped his mother's skirt with both hands.

She tightened her hold on her husband.

He grabbed the turnip leaves.
"Everyone ready?" he said. "Now,
one, two, three... **heeeeeeave!**"

And they heaved and tugged and heaved some more, until they were red in the face. But still the turnip didn't move.

With a "Woof!" the farmer's dog
bounded into the field.

"Let's... try... again..." gasped the farmer. The dog caught hold of Jack's shirt with his paws.

Jack pulled on his mother's skirt

She hugged the farmer and the farmer gripped the turnip leaves.

Heeeeeeave!

The turnip did not move at all.

On silent paws, the cat crept up...

Nip! She bit the dog's tail. The dog yowled and jumped in pain.

The dog jerked away from Jack, ripping his shirt...

Jack lost his balance and yanked on his mother's skirt, which came away in his hands...

She squealed and let go of the farmer...

The farmer let go of the turnip leaves...

...and they all
fell flat on their backs.

55

The farmer brushed the dirt off his clothes. "Let's try this one more time," he said. "We can't be beaten by a turnip!"

I'm
hungry.

As he spoke, a bird
flew past.

Tweet,
tweet!

The bird pecked the cat's tail with its beak.

The cat clamped the dog's tail between her teeth.

The dog gripped Jack's shirt with his paws.

Jack held onto his mother's torn skirt. She hugged the farmer.

The farmer grabbed the turnip and everybody tugged.

They tugged and tugged and tugged
and tugged, until...

Slowly,

slowly,

very, very

slowly,

the turnip began to move.

"It's **big**," said the farmer.

"It's **huge**," said his wife.

"It's enormous!"

cried Jack.

Woof!

Meow!

Tweet!

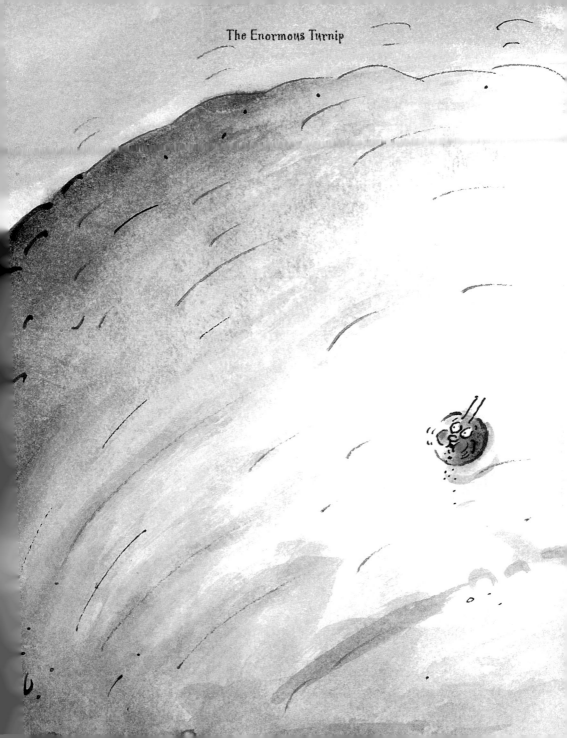

It had taken them hours, but, at last, the turnip was out of the ground.

The Enormous Turnip

The farmer was delighted. "I said it couldn't beat us," he declared, and yawned.

That night, he fell asleep with a smile on his face.

The next morning, Jack and his mother got to work, chopping up the turnip.

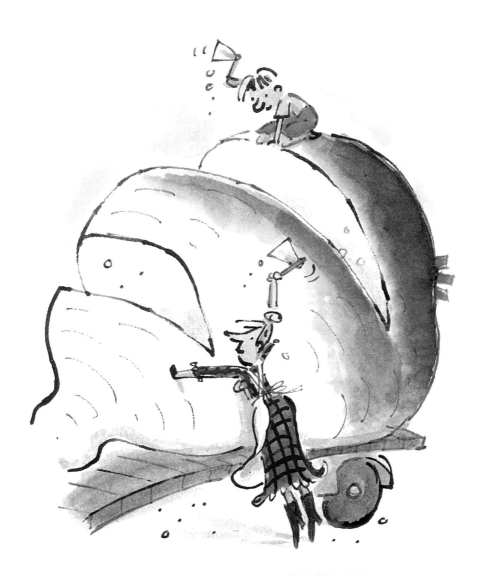

That day, they ate turnip soup
for lunch...

...and turnip
soup for
supper.

In fact, they had turnip soup for breakfast, lunch and supper every day for a month.

Turnip Jam

Turnip Soup

Turnip Jam

"Next year, I'm growing carrots,"
said the farmer.

Danny the Dragon

On the edge of some deep, dark woods, beside a tiny village, lived a bright green dragon named Danny.
Some dragons are scary...

...but not Danny.

Each morning, he wandered down to the village to greet his friends as they shopped in the market.

Everyone was used to seeing the friendly dragon around the place, so they didn't bat an eyelid.

Danny liked to help the villagers whenever he could. And he had one particular talent that he put to good use.

Morning, Peg!
Morning, Sam!

Every night, he visited each house in the village. Joe's cottage was first.

Danny leaned over his friend's fireplace. Then, whoosh! With one blast from Danny's fiery breath, the old man's fire crackled to life.

Ah, lovely and warm. Thanks, Danny.

Next stop was Peg and her family. With Danny's help, their dinner was cooked in no time.

At Sam's house, Danny was able to light three candles all at once. In an instant, the entire room was aglow.

Thanks,
Danny.

Once he'd visited everyone, Danny
could go back to his house in the woods
feeling happy with himself.

One day, a brightly painted
wagon trundled into the village.
It was driven by a tall
stranger in fancy
clothes.

"Roll up, roll up!" cried the man.
"Come and buy Mr. Marvo's magic fire
sticks. Only a penny each."

The villagers had never seen magic fire sticks before. They gathered around excitedly as Mr. Marvo unloaded his wagon.

"What do they do?" asked Joe.
"Allow me to demonstrate," said
Mr. Marvo. "Stand back, ladies and
gentlemen, and prepare to be amazed."

Mr. Marvo grabbed a fire stick and aimed it at a pile of logs. Next second, a jet of magical stars shot out. "They light your fires when you're cold," he cried.

"That's not all," added Mr. Marvo. "When you're hungry, they can cook your food."

"And they can light your candles when it gets dark," declared the salesman, as a bolt of blue stars whizzed around a street lamp.

"My magnificent, magical fire sticks make life easy!"

Whoosh!

Wonderful!

The villagers were impressed. They took out their money and surged around Mr. Marvo's wagon.

In less than five minutes, Mr. Marvo's entire stock of fire sticks was sold out.

Danny knew nothing about what had
happened that day. As night fell, he
trotted into the village as usual.

He went to Joe's cottage and popped his head through the door. "Shall I light your fire?" he asked.

"No thanks, Danny," replied the old man. "I've got these new-fangled magic fire sticks now. I don't need a dragon any more."

"Um, okay," said Danny. He didn't know what else to say. So he left Joe and walked along the street. "I'm sure Peg will need my help," he thought.

He knocked on Peg's door. As it opened, a spicy, tasty smell wafted out into the night air. "Evening, Peg," said Danny. "Shall I cook your supper?"

"Not tonight thanks, Danny," replied
Peg. "The sausages are already cooked,
and the wild boar is on its way."

"Magic fire sticks again," sighed Danny, as he left Peg to her meal. "Oh well, perhaps Sam still needs me."

He plodded up to Sam's house and gently rattled the door handle.

"I don't suppose you have any candles that need lighting, Sam?" asked Danny, as his old friend appeared.

Sam's reply came as no surprise.

"Sorry, Danny," he said. "This magic
fire stick did the job tonight. Why not
try one of the other villagers? Someone's
bound to need your help."

But it was the same story at every house. Everybody had Mr. Marvo's magic fire sticks. Nobody needed Danny's fire-breathing skills.

"No one wants me any more," sniffed Danny sadly, as he slowly headed home.

"Maybe I won't bother to visit the village again," he thought to himself. He trudged back to his tumbledown home in the woods and tried not to cry.

Meanwhile, on the other side of the village, a band of robbers was passing by. "That looks a likely spot for rich pickings," smirked Knuckles, their leader.

They noticed the wisps of smoke coming from the chimneys. "Look! Somewhere to warm our freezing bones," said Toothy.

They saw the bright lights streaming
through the windows. "And plenty of
candles to brighten up our gloomy
hideout," said Stinker.

Then they smelled sizzling sausages.
"Mmm, and lots of yummy grub for our
rumbling tummies," sighed Nosey.

"What are we waiting for?" cried
Knuckles. "Charge!"

The gang raced down the hill and stormed into the village. Then they split up and barged their way into the locals' homes. No one was safe.

"Step aside, grandpa!" cried Knuckles, pushing Joe away from his fire.

"We need this more than you," chuckled Nosey, warming his hands.

"You big bullies!" croaked Joe.

"Grub's up!" yelled Toothy, as he shoved Peg's family away from their supper.

"Time you all went on a diet," laughed Stinker.

"You greedy thieves!" cried Peg.

"Keep your pooch out of our way!" shouted Wrinkly, as Tubs stuffed Sam's candles into a sack.

"Hope you're not scared of the dark, mister," laughed Tubs.

The robbers went from house to house causing chaos.

"Who can help us?" cried the villagers.

"Yikes, not me!" squeaked Mr. Marvo pathetically, and he ran out of the village as fast as he could.

In the woods, Danny woke with a start. He heard the cries of the villagers in the distance.

"Somebody help!" they called desperately. "Save us from the robbers!"

Quick as a flash, Danny thundered into the village. He soon spotted the thieves with their plunder.

"Hee hee!" chortled Toothy. "That was a good night's work."

Danny rushed up to Toothy and Wrinkly. Before they knew what was happening, he set their beards alight.

Ooch!

Ow!

"A d..d..dragon!" yowled Toothy, as his filthy beard went up in flames.

Danny let out a stream of fire, and Tubs and Nosey found their toes toasted.

"H...help!" wailed Tubs, as his shoe burst into flames in front of him.

Stinker and Knuckles made a run for it. But Danny was too quick for them. He took a deep breath and blasted their bottoms.

The gang sprinted out of the village in a cloud of smoke. "Don't let the dragon get us!" they pleaded.

The crooks disappeared over the horizon and were never seen again.

"Thank you, Danny," said Joe. "We didn't realize how much we needed you." "Three cheers for Danny!" cried Peg.

The thankful villagers gave Danny his job back. And they found a much better use for Mr. Marvo's magic sticks.

The Inch Prince

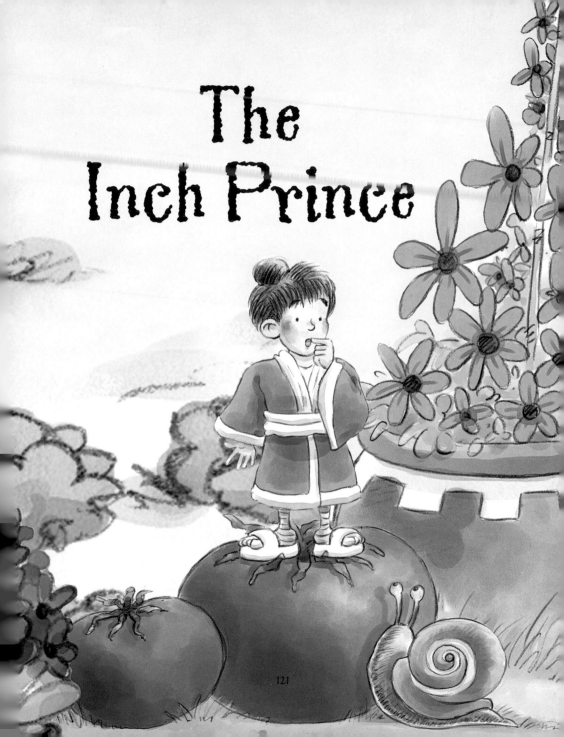

Long ago, in a remote village in Japan, there lived an old couple named Mr. and Mrs. Ping.

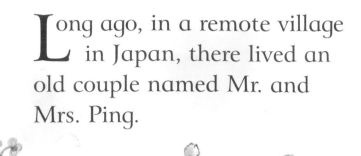

Their home was a tiny house at the foot of a mountain, beside a rushing river.

The Pings loved it.

Every day, Mr. Ping weeded the
beans and the rest of the plants in their
vegetable plot.

Meanwhile,
Mrs. Ping fed the
chickens and all
their other animals.

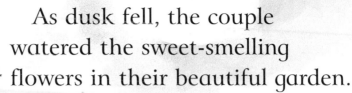

As dusk fell, the couple
watered the sweet-smelling
flowers in their beautiful garden.

The Pings had everything they could
possibly want... well, almost.

"I wish we had some children," sighed Mrs. Ping sadly, one evening.

"So do I," said Mr. Ping. "But only a teeny child could fit in our tiny house. We hardly have room for the cat."

"Small things can be special too," said his wife.

"Maybe," said Mr. Ping, "but they'd need to be the smallest child in the world to fit in here."

"I wouldn't care if they were just one inch tall," said Mrs. Ping.

At that very moment, a fairy
happened to fly past. She overheard
what Mr. and Mrs. Ping were saying.

She noticed their healthy, plump vegetables growing away in the sun.

Not to mention their contented animals...

and their enormous blossoming flowers.

"These two are obviously very good at looking after everything around them," thought the fairy. "They deserve to be looked after too."

With that, she hovered over the Pings' tiny house, waved her wand and whispered some magic words.

Jumping beans and
flying fish,
Give these folk their
dearest wish.

Soon afterwards, Mr. and Mrs. Ping became the proud parents of a teeny weeny boy.

In fact, he was so teeny, he was just one inch tall!

Well, we wanted a small child.

Isn't he sweet?

"Let's name him Issun-boshi," said Mrs. Ping. "It means 'one inch boy'."

"And we could call him Issy, for short," said her husband. "Um, very short," he added with a smile.

Time passed quickly for the Pings
and their new son. Each year, their
vegetables grew more plump.

Their animals
grew bigger and
fatter.

And their flowers
grew so tall they
almost fell over.

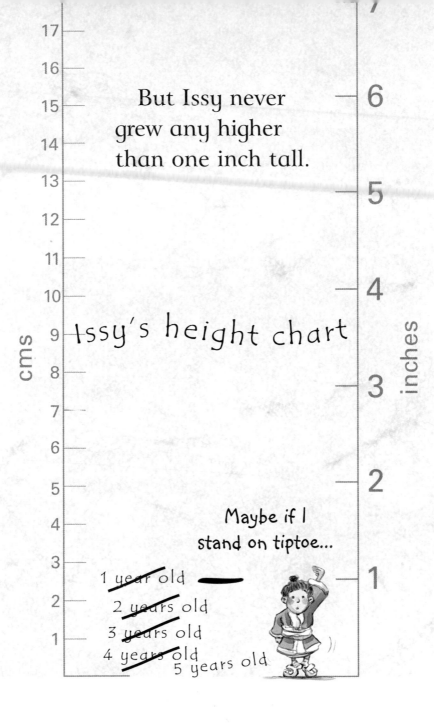

But Issy never
grew any higher
than one inch tall.

Issy's height chart

Maybe if I
stand on tiptoe...

1 year old
2 years old
3 years old
4 years old
5 years old

cms

17
16
15
14
13
12
11
10
9
8
7
6
5
4
3
2
1

inches

7
6
5
4
3
2
1

Issy was so tiny, the Pings had to find new uses for everyday objects.

A bottle top from Mr. Ping's home-made rice wine became a bathtub.

One of the shoelaces from Mrs. Ping's pink walking boots was turned into a scarf.

A dried pea made
a great ball.

Goal!

Mrs. Ping's button
collection was put to good use
as dinner plates.

And every night, Issy
curled up to sleep in his
little matchbox bed.

Zzzzzzzzzz

When he was eighteen years old, it was time for Issy to leave home.

"I'll get a job in the city," he announced confidently.

His parents gave him three presents for his journey. He had a rice bowl for a boat...

two wooden chopsticks, which made a fine pair of oars...

...and a sword to defend himself – actually, Mrs. Ping's sharpest needle.

around wild woods...

and through
walled market
towns...

...until he reached
the bustling
big city.

Issy clambered ashore and scuttled along the crowded streets. "I'll ask the emperor for a job," he thought.

"That's if I don't get squashed first."

After dodging hundreds of stomping feet, Issy finally reached the emperor's enormous palace.

He strode up to the guards on the gate.

Issy puffed out his chest. "I'd like a job," he declared, politely but firmly.

The guards looked down and laughed.

"You're teeny," said one with a chuckle. "What could a pipsqueak like *you* do?"

"I can run past you for a start," said Issy.

Hey! Where did he go?

He jumped over the guard's foot and darted into the palace before anyone could stop him.

In the courtyard, a maid was busy washing the royal clothes.

"I'd like a job," said Issy.

"Hee hee, you're weeny," chuckled the maid. "What can *you* do?"

"I can run past you for a start," Issy replied.

Hey! Where did he go?

He jumped over the maid's soap and sprinted into the palace kitchen.

A cook was preparing
the royal dinner.

"I'd like a job,"
said Issy.

"Ha!" snorted the cook, as he stirred
a pot of squelchy cabbage. "You're tiny.
What can *you* do?"

"I can run past you for a start," answered Issy with a grin.

He swerved around the cook's oven and dashed into the next room.

Issy gasped. He'd arrived in the throne room. He bowed respectfully to the emperor and the princess.

"I'd like a job, please," said Issy.

"Would you, now?"
said the emperor.

"He's teeny-weeny, Daddy," said
Princess Chi-Chi. "What can *he* do?"

"Well, I ran past your guard, your maid and your cook to get here," said Issy proudly. "They couldn't stop me."

The emperor thought for a moment. "You can look after Princess Chi-Chi," he said. "She needs a bodyguard."

"But Daddy," moaned the princess. "How could he defend me? He's only one inch tall."

"Small things can be special too," said the emperor wisely. "You're hired."

"Thank you, Your Majesty," said Issy.

From then on, Issy never
left the princess's side.
He was there in
the morning.

He was
there in the
afternoon.

He was even
there all night.

One day, the princess left the
palace to visit her aunt, far
beyond the city. As usual,
Issy was right by her side.

Palace ▲

After many miles, they came
to a dark forest. "I'm s...scared,"
said Princess Chi-Chi.

"I'll look after you," said Issy.
"What could *you* do?"
quivered the princess.

Just then, a terrifying roar echoed around the wood.

RAAAGGGHH!

A giant ogre crashed through the trees. He reached out to grab the princess.

"Put her down!" shouted Issy with all his might. "Or I'll..."

"You?" grunted the ogre. "What could *you* do?"

With that, the ogre scooped up Issy. "Mmm, I love bite-size snacks," he said and popped Issy in his mouth.

Issy thought quickly. He took his needle-sword and pricked the ogre's tongue. The ogre let out an ear-splitting howl.

OOOOWWWW!

The ogre spat out Issy and ran off into the woods. "That'll teach him," cried the tiny bodyguard.

"Thank you, Issy," said the princess. "You saved my life."

"Hey, look!" said Issy. "The ogre left his hammer behind."

"The legends say that an ogre's hammer is magic," said the princess excitedly. She tried to pick up the massive tool, but it was far too heavy.

"I wish you were bigger, Issy," she puffed. "Then maybe you could lift it."

Instantly, a cloud of magical stars shot out of the hammer and swept around Issy.

"W...what's going on?" he cried.

Issy felt something
strange happening.
His arms seemed
to be getting
longer, and his
legs, in fact
his whole
body was
getting
bigger...

and bigger...

and bigger...

Seconds later, he found himself standing shoulder to shoulder with the princess for the very first time.

"I'm as tall as you!" cried Issy. "The hammer must have granted your wish."

The princess fell in love with Issy, but not because he was tall. She loved him because he was brave.

It wasn't long before they got married and lived in a house next to the palace.

The house was small, but Prince Issy and Princess Chi-Chi were happy.

They both knew that small things can be special too.

Androcles and the Lion

A long time ago, there lived a man named Androcles. He was so poor, all he had to eat was one measly piece of bread a day.

But, because he was kind, he always shared what little he had with his friends.

Androcles worked as a slave in a big villa near the city of Rome. The villa belonged to a rich and lazy man named Brutus Flabbicus.

Brutus worked his
slaves hard. Every day,
Androcles had to scrub
the villa steps...

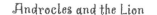

mop all the floors...

You missed a
spot, clumsy!

make all the beds...

sweat
over a hot
stove...

serve what felt
like hundreds of
meals...

and spend all evening
up to his elbows in
dirty dishes.

Androcles didn't think things could get any worse. He was wrong. Brutus began feeding him stale bread to save money.

"Even the birds won't eat it," sighed Androcles. "And I don't blame them."

"There's only one thing left to do," he thought. "I'll have to run away."

That night, he waited until Brutus was asleep. Then he sneaked out of the villa and ran into the forest.

Androcles had never been in the forest before. Spooky eyes stared out at him from the creepy shadows.

Suddenly, he heard a gruff, snarling noise coming from behind a bush.

Androcles felt a shiver run up his spine. "Wh... who's there?" he croaked nervously, as he crept closer and closer.

Carefully, he peered around the bush
and came face to face with a huge
lion. The beast let out a loud roar and
Androcles ran for cover.

RAAAAGGGGH!

But to Androcles' surprise, the lion didn't run after him. He just sat where he was, as still as a statue.

"That's odd," thought Androcles. He was so puzzled, he cautiously tiptoed back. "Um, why didn't you chase me?" he asked timidly.

"I can't run," sniffed the lion. "I can't even walk. I was out for a stroll when I got this thorn stuck in my paw. It stings like crazy."

"You poor thing," said Androcles. "Let me see if I can take it out for you."

Androcles took hold of the lion's paw and gripped the thorn. "This might hurt a little," he warned.

I can't bear to look.

"Just do it quickly, please," pleaded the lion. Androcles tugged out the thorn as fast as he could.

"Ooooch!" yelped the lion.

"All done," said Androcles, waving the thorn under the lion's nose.

"Whew!" puffed the lion. "That feels so much better. Thanks for helping me out. My name's Leo, by the way."

"And I'm Androcles."

The lion smiled and gave his rescuer a big, sloppy lick.

Slluuuurp!

"Hey, that tickles," laughed Androcles. From then on, he and Leo were the best of friends.

A snug cave in
the middle of the
forest became their
new home.

Each morning, Leo
went out into the forest
looking for food.

There were plenty of
juicy berries and crunchy
nuts to be found if you knew where
to look.

Leo brought
the food back to
Androcles, who
turned it into
delicious meals.

One day, Androcles was enjoying his morning walk, when he saw a stranger.

"That's odd," thought Androcles. "Hardly anyone comes into the forest." He crept closer to get a better look.

As Androcles got nearer, he recognized the man's uniform. "A soldier!" he thought, with a shiver. "What's he doing around here?"

The soldier unrolled some paper. Androcles gasped when he saw what was written on it.

WANTED
for running away

Andrscles

Ha ha! He won't be
free for much longer.

As Androcles watched in horror, he
felt a bug land on his nose. It tickled so
much, he couldn't stop himself from...

Atishoooooooo!

"Hey, you!" cried the soldier in surprise. "What are you doing sneaking around this forest?"

"I, er, um..." stuttered Androcles.

"Just a second," said the soldier. "I recognize you. You're the escaped slave!"

Who, me? No way. Bye!

"Stop in the name of the emperor!" yelled the soldier, drawing his sword.

As the soldier chased him,
Androcles felt his heart
thumping through his chest.
But he dared not stop.

The soldier chased
him up hills...

down hills...

across a raging, rushing river...

in between mighty pine trees...

until finally, Androcles ran out of puff and collapsed in a sweaty heap.

"Gotcha!" cried the soldier with glee. He pulled Androcles to his feet and dragged him to a nearby cart.

"Are you taking me back to Brutus?" panted Androcles, as the soldier threw him on board.

"You should be so lucky," laughed the soldier, locking him in place. "You're going to Rome, Andy my boy."

"What for?" asked Androcles.

"You'll see," the soldier replied as he took the reins. With that, they were off.

Androcles had an uncomfortable, bumpy ride to Rome. When he arrived, he found the city heaving with bustling, noisy crowds.

He'd never seen so many people in one place before.

"What's that big, round building?"
he asked.

"It's the arena," replied the soldier.

Androcles didn't like the look of it.
"What happens there?" he asked.

"You'll soon see," smirked the soldier.

The cart trundled up to the arena.
A man called Clinkus appeared and
unlocked Androcles.

Clinkus led Androcles into the arena,
past a cage of lions.

These animals weren't as gentle as Leo.

ROAR! SNARL!

Yikes!

"What are they doing here?" Androcles asked nervously.

"You'll see," said Clinkus, with a grin.

Androcles was thrown into a dingy prison cell with a man named Marco.

"What happens now?" asked Androcles. "We fight in the middle of the arena," said Marco.

"But I don't want to fight you,"
said Androcles.

"We don't fight each other..."
Marco sighed.

"We fight the lions."

Androcles gulped. He didn't think much of his chances against one of those fierce animals he'd seen earlier.

We'll be torn to pieces!

"Everyone in Rome comes to watch," said Marco. "Even the emperor."

"Our fights are tomorrow afternoon," he added. "I suppose we better get some rest, while we can."

But Androcles and Marco didn't get much sleep that night.

The next afternoon came all too quickly. Clinkus arrived and took Androcles from his cell.

It's show time, skinny!

He dragged him down a long, dark tunnel to a doorway.

Clinkus unlocked the door and shoved
Androcles out into the sunlight.

Put up a
good fight!

As Androcles struggled to his feet,
he realized he was in the middle of the
dreaded arena.

Androcles gasped as he caught sight of the lions waiting to be unleashed.

A gate opened in a side wall, and
an enormous lion charged out.
Androcles trembled
with fear. There was
nowhere to run.

Androcles fell to his knees and closed his eyes. "I only hope it's over quickly," he thought. He could feel the lion's breath on the back of his neck.

Suddenly, Androcles felt a lick on his hand. He opened his eyes to see... Leo!

Hello Androcles. Nice to see you again.

"I was caught last night," explained Leo. "They brought me here to fight."

Androcles hugged his friend. No one in the arena could believe their eyes.

"Androcles has tamed the lion," cried the crowd. "What a hero!" They began chanting his name.

Androcles! Androcles! Androcles!

Clinkus took Androcles to the emperor.

"I've never seen such bravery," said the emperor. "In fact, I'm so impressed, I've decided to set you free."

Androcles thought of his friends. "Please will you free my cell mate Marco and the lion too?" he asked.

The emperor smiled. "Very well," he said. Moments later, Androcles and Marco were reunited.

My hero!

Androcles and his friends decided to leave Rome and start their own show...

...where no one ever had to fight.

Come and see
the friendly lion.

Buy your tickets
here!

216

Stone Soup

There was once a poor man named Wilf. He would travel from town to town looking for work, with only his dog, Scruff, and a very special stone.

One day, he came to a
small cream cottage with a thatched roof.
"Let's try here," he said to Scruff and
rapped on the door.

Knock!
Knock!

It was opened by a woman who gave him a suspicious look. "Who are you?" she snapped. "What do you want?"

"Good morning ma'am," said Wilf. "I was wondering if you had any small jobs I could do, in return for some lunch?"

"I'm sorry, I don't have any jobs," said the woman, starting to close the door.

"I can make soup from a stone," Wilf said, quickly.

Wilf reached into his pocket and took out a shiny stone. "This stone," he said, "will make the most delicious soup you have ever tasted."

He waited for the water to steam and then dropped the stone into the pot.

The soup began to boil and bubble.
Wilf dipped in a spoon and tasted it.
"Mmm, not bad," he said.

"It tastes pretty good," he went on,
"but I think an onion would make
it better."

"Well, I have onions," said the old woman. And she put four on the kitchen table and sliced them swiftly.

A sharp, oniony smell filled the room. The old woman scooped up the onion slices and dropped them into the pot.

Wilf let the soup bubble for a little longer. Then he dipped in his spoon and tasted it again. "Mmm, getting tasty," he said.

He pointed to a sack of potatoes on the wall. "Perhaps a potato...?"

"What a good idea!" said the woman.

She lifted the sack from the wall, took out six large potatoes and peeled them.

Then *snick! snack! snick! snack!* She chopped the potatoes into neat squares...

...scooped up the glistening cubes and dropped them into the pot.

The soup bubbled. Wilf dipped his spoon in a third time and slurped a mouthful. "Mmmm!"

"It's tasting wonderful now," he said. "But it needs a little something else..."

He spotted a string of plump sausages hanging above the fire and licked his lips.

"Sausages would be perfect!" he said.

So the old woman unhooked several sausages and chopped those up too. As she added them to the pot, Wilf smiled. A rich, meaty smell drifted up.

"I think it's ready!" said Wilf.

The old woman found some bowls and a ladle, and Wilf served two very generous helpings.

"Stone soup really *is* delicious!" said the old woman. "I think your stone must be magic."

Wilf smiled. He fished in the pot for his stone, spooned it out, washed it and put it back in his pocket.

"It is a magical stone," Wilf agreed with a wink. "Wherever I go with it, I am never hungry."

"Would you like to stay for supper?"
said the woman. "There's plenty of
stone soup."

The Clumsy Crocodile

Cassy Green was on her way to work.
It was the very first day of her new
job. She was going to work at Everglades,
the biggest and best store in town.

It sold things you just couldn't buy anywhere else. So, when Cassy got a job there, she was as pleased as punch.

- Toy Department
- China Department
- Exotic Pet Department
- Robot Department
- Luxury Goods Department
- Food Hall

First, Cassy was sent to work in the China Department. After only ten minutes, she had sold sixty cups and saucers to a very rich lady. She was doing well.

Cassy packed the china carefully into a box. She was as gentle as a crocodile can be, but maybe just a little slow. The lady began to get impatient.

Cassy quickly tied a big bow on the box. She didn't want the lady to be cross, not her very first customer. But as Cassy picked up the box, disaster struck!

Now be careful!

She'd packed it upside down. Sixty
cups and saucers smashed onto the floor.
The customer stamped her foot angrily
and left.

Oops!

CRASH

249

Next, Cassy was sent to the Toy Department. She hoped there was less to break. She didn't want any more accidents.

"I must put this ball away," she thought. "Someone could trip over it and have a bad fall."

But as she bent down, her tail swung out behind her. The Toytown Express was knocked right off its rails.

So she was sent to the Food Hall. But there, things went from bad to worse.

Cassy tripped over a stool. A bowl of salad flew into the air and landed...

...on Ernest Everglade's head.

Ernest Everglade owned the department store. He was Cassy's boss and he was not a happy man.

"Go to my office," he yelled. "NOW!"
Trembling, Cassy obeyed.

Ernest Everglade was furious. "I like salad," he fumed. "But not on my head!"

"Go away and don't ever come back," he shouted. "Everglades is the biggest and best store in town. We don't want clumsy crocodiles here. You've caused far too much trouble already."

Cassy was heartbroken.

"Just give me one more chance," she begged. "I promise I'll be careful. I'll be as quiet as a mouse, as gentle as a giraffe..."

But Mr. Everglade was more interested in his newspaper. He wasn't even listening to Cassy.

The Clumsy Crocodile

At last, he looked up. "Are you still here? I have more important things to worry about. Some jewel thieves are in town – the famous Greedy Boys."

Cassy gasped. Everyone had heard of the Greedy Boys. But she still wanted her job back. She began to cry.

Now, Mr. Everglade couldn't stand crying. He would do anything to stop it.

"OK, OK," he said. "Go to the Luxury Goods Department first thing Monday morning."

Oh thank you! You won't regret it. I promise.

On Sunday, Cassy worked hard at home, getting ready for Monday.

She emptied her cupboards and stacked everything inside them. She stacked every pot, plate, cup and saucer in the house.

The stacks got wobblier and higher...
but they didn't fall down.

"Ooh!" cried Cassy. "Perhaps my
clumsiness is cured?"

Next she found paper, scissors, ribbon and tape. She wrapped everything she could get her hands on.

Why are
balls so round?

When she'd finished wrapping, Cassy was exhausted. All she wanted to do was sit down.

But when she looked for her comfiest chair, there was just one small problem...

So she set up her mirror and served imaginary customers.

"A flying pig? Try the pet department sir... I'm sorry, madam, we don't sell crocodile-skin handbags.

You don't like your spotted socks, sir? I'll change them at once.

That looks heavy. Let me carry that priceless statue for you..."

And she smiled her toothy crocodile smile until her whole face ached.

Can I help you?

Finally, Cassy put
on her Everglades
badge and
admired herself
in the mirror.

Mr. Everglade
will be proud
of me.

"I look perfect! I'm going to be the best sales assistant Everglades has ever had," she said proudly.

On Monday morning, Cassy was the first to arrive in the Luxury Goods Department.

She tiptoed past the jewels and gems and antique pots, her tail trembling in trepidation.

Only the security guard was there. He had been guarding the store during the night.

The guard was finishing his breakfast. He was very pleased to see Cassy. "I'm glad you're here," he said. "Now I can go home to bed."

I'll be off now then.

"No!" cried Cassy. "Don't leave me alone in the store! I'm not ready for that yet. Why don't you stay a little while longer? I'll make you tea..."

Please don't go!

"You'll be fine," said the guard. "Just keep an eye on the Everglades Emerald."

The guard left. Cassy wasn't nervous any more. She felt important. She was in charge.

Don't worry. You can count on me.

The Everglades Emerald was the most expensive thing in the store. It was kept in a case of extra strong glass. Cassy gazed at it in wide-eyed wonder.

"Wow!" she gasped. "It's beautiful."

"I know!" she thought. "I'll polish the glass, to make it even sparklier."

But Cassy wasn't the only one admiring the emerald...

Hiding behind a pot were Nigel and Rupert – the Greedy Boys!

"What a beauty," sighed Nigel. "I can't wait to get my hands on it. That emerald will make us millions."

"But look at its case," said Rupert.
"How will we ever break the glass?"

"Never fear," Nigel whispered.
And as Cassy wandered away from
the emerald, Nigel took something from
his pocket.

He held up a small whistle.
"You imbecile! How's that going to help us?" scoffed Rupert.

"Wait and see. It's my secret weapon," said Nigel. "It can't be heard by humans, but it can..."

He put the whistle to his lips and blew. The case exploded.

"...shatter glass!" he finished.

He grinned. The Everglades Emerald was theirs for the taking.

"At last!" gasped Rupert. "The emerald is ours!"

Nigel and Rupert sneaked
out from their hiding place.
Their eyes glittered
with greed.

"Now to
collect our
prize," said
Nigel.

The thieves crept closer to the emerald. But Nigel had made a big mistake.

He was right about humans not being able to hear his whistle. What he didn't know was that animals could hear it...

THE EVERGLADES EMERALD

282

"Hey!" thought Cassy. "The Toytown Express!" She spun around, ready to race to the Toy Department... forgetting her tail, which swung around too.

This time it hooked a priceless pearl necklace.

Cassy tugged her tail and... the necklace snapped.

Oops!

The pearls went flying. So did Cassy. She knocked over a glass cabinet.

China plates smashed. Golden objects crashed. The pearls rolled across the floor.

They rolled right under the feet of the Greedy Boys, sending them skidding to the floor. The Everglades Emerald came tumbling after them.

Cassy turned to see the Greedy Boys lying in a heap.

"Oh no! Customers!" she cried and rushed over to help them up.

Please let me help. I am so sorry.

Rupert was groaning in agony. Nigel
still had his eye on the emerald. He
wouldn't let a clumsy crocodile ruin
his plans. Not now
he was this close to
his prize.

It can still
be mine. It has
to be!

In her hurry to help, Cassy tripped. She slid across the floor, her arms thrust out. She flew past the Greedy Boys.

Oops!

"Aaargh!" she screamed, as she realized she was going to crash, nose-first, with a table...

...a table which held Everglades' precious Ancient Treasures.

The table wobbled. The treasures wobbled...

Then they crashed to the floor.

Cassy got up. She was horrified. What had she done?

One of the ancient pots had toppled off the table...

...straight onto her customers' heads.
"I'm finished," thought Cassy.

At that moment, the boss walked in.

Cassy started to explain.

"I was going to polish... there was a noise... my t-t-tail... It got c-c-caught. Then I slid..."

But Mr. Everglade wasn't listening. He was gazing at the ground and his face was turning red.

I'm so
s-s-s-sorry.

He had just seen the Everglades
Emerald lying on the floor.

"What's that doing here?" he cried.
"Our most prized possession! Our
precious gem!"

Then he saw the pot. And the legs. And the bag lying next to them. And he quickly put two and two together.

He was no longer a cross boss. He was a very pleased and excited boss.

He picked up the emerald and beamed at Cassy.

"Well done! You've saved the Everglades Emerald."

Cassy was puzzled. Mr. Everglade pointed to the pot.

"And you've caught the Greedy Boys," he added.

Faint groans could be heard from underneath the pot.

"Oh? So I have!" said Cassy. She felt very pleased with herself.

That afternoon Mr. Everglade
gave a party for Cassy. The
whole town was invited.

"Three cheers for Cassy the
crocodile!" they cried.

Nigel and Rupert watched the party too... from behind bars.

"Caught by a crocodile," groaned Nigel. "I can't believe it!"

Cassy thought it was the best party ever. There was singing and dancing, cake and ice cream – and fantastic fizzing fireworks.

Then Cassy was given a medal. It was the proudest moment of her life. She was a hero.

After the party, Mr. Everglade smiled at Cassy.

"I've got a new job for you," he said. He didn't want Cassy to be an assistant any more.

Instead, she became Everglades' Chief Taster and Tester – with her tail tucked firmly beneath her.

The Sorcerer's Apprentice

Max was an apprentice. Sticklewick the sorcerer had promised to teach him magic, but so far all Max seemed to do was clean. He had spent the entire morning cleaning the workshop – and he still hadn't finished.

Mop this... Polish that... I'm fed up with it.

"How will I ever learn to be a sorcerer like Sticklewick?" he moaned. "He never lets me do any magic."

Just then, Max heard footsteps on the stone staircase. "Uh-oh, that's him! Back to work."

A moment later, Sticklewick appeared.
"Max, I have to go into town," he
announced, waving a long shopping list.

"I used the last of the dragons' eggs yesterday, I ran out of newts' blood the day before and we're completely out of goblins' toenails."

Hmm... Maybe I'll get a tube of pixies' earwax, too.

Max was delighted. Sticklewick had never left him alone in the castle before.

Yippee! A free afternoon!

"I can explore the dungeons and swim in the moat," he thought. "Or just sit in the sun and do nothing at all."

"There's plenty to do while I'm out," Sticklewick went on. "For a start, this floor could do with a good scrub."

Look! I've just stepped on a toadstool.

"But fill up the water tank first. It's almost empty."

Max groaned. It always took hours to fetch enough water to fill the tank. And it was such hard work.

Rats! There goes my free afternoon.

That should keep him out of mischief.

"Oh, one more thing," Sticklewick added. "Don't try any spells!" He frowned.

"Or I'll... I'll turn you into a tadpole," he threatened, his bushy eyebrows bristling.

With that, there was a flash of light and a puff of purple smoke. The sorcerer was gone.

"Well, don't just stand there!" croaked a little voice. "You have work to do." It was Tabitha, Sticklewick's toad.

"Oh, hop it!" said Max, crossly. "I've been working hard all morning. I need a rest first."

"There's no need to be rude," said Tabitha, hopping onto a broomstick.

Max didn't reply. Seeing Tabitha perched on the broom had given him a brilliant idea.

Last week, Sticklewick had cast a spell on a broomstick. It had come to life and done everything the sorcerer asked.

"I'm sure I can remember the words," Max thought, concentrating.

How hard
can it be?

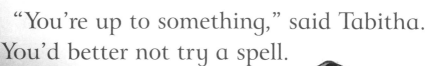

"You're up to something," said Tabitha.
"You'd better not try a spell.
You heard Sticklewick."

"Don't be such a spoilsport,"
said Max. "What harm can it do?
Anyway, he won't know."

Max closed his eyes and thought for a moment. Taking a deep breath, he said the magic words...

Root and branch of old oak tree, bring this broom to life for me!

All at once, the broom began to twitch. It shook and it shuddered, then... slowly... it grew two skinny arms and two skinny legs.

Wow!
I did it!

"Now," Max ordered the broom, "fetch me some water. And be quick about it!"

The broom ran off. In no time, Max heard it coming tap-tap-tap down the steps. It poured the water into the tank and set off for more.

Feeling very pleased with himself, Max flopped down in the sorcerer's chair. "Time for a snooze," he yawned. Soon, he was fast asleep.

Max woke up to find Tabitha hopping on his lap. "What is it?" he mumbled, sleepily.

"Get up! Get up! Get up! Get up!" she croaked, jumping up and down.

"It's a disaster," she explained. "The tank is overflowing and the broom won't stop!"

Max leaped up. Water was sloshing over the sides of the tank and the broom was clattering down the steps again.

"Stop!" he shouted. "That's enough!"
But the broom took no notice. Streams
of water poured across the floor.

Oh no!
Now what?

"Great stuttering sorcerers, just say the spell!" begged Tabitha.

"What spell?" asked Max, puzzled. Then he remembered. Of course! He needed a spell to make the broom stop.

"Oh no," he groaned. "I... um... I don't think I actually know it."

Oh boy!

By now, the water was ankle deep. And still the broom was fetching more.

"I know!" cried Max, splashing across the floor. "I'll look in Sticklewick's spell book. Let's see…" Max flicked through page after page.

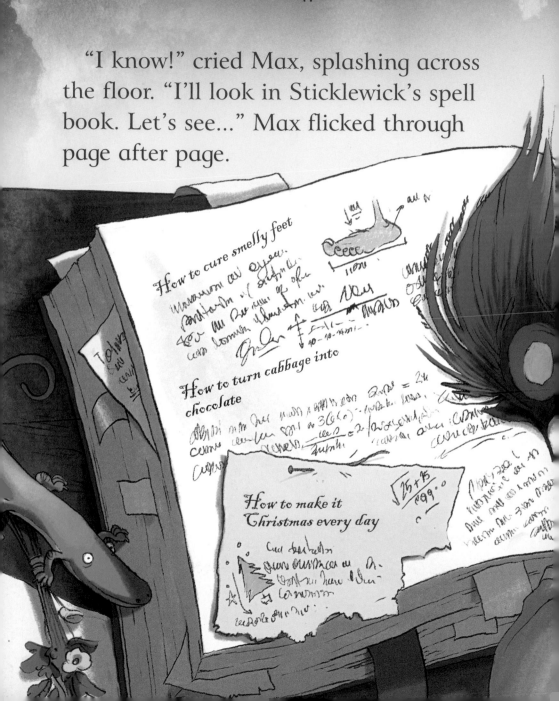

How to cure smelly feet

How to turn cabbage into chocolate

How to make it Christmas every day

"This is hopeless," he wailed. "There are thousands of spells here. I'll *never* find the right one. What am I going to do?"

"You could chop the broom up," said Tabitha, helpfully.

"Good thinking!" said Max. He grabbed a hatchet, lifted it high above his head and swung it down hard.

With a loud CRACK, the broomstick split in two.

"That was close," said Max, with a sigh of relief. "Thanks Tabitha, you're brilliant! Tabitha? What's wrong?"

Tabitha was gazing in horror at the broomstick halves. "Just look," she croaked.

Max's eyes opened wide. The two pieces of the broom were moving... and each piece was growing new arms and legs.

Faster than ever, the brooms raced off for more water.

"I'm in big trouble now," thought Max, glumly.

In no time, the brooms were back, sloshing water everywhere.

Max did everything he could think of to try and stop them.

He tried tripping them.

He even tried to sit on them. But it was no use.

"I give up," said Max, miserably. "Sticklewick is going to be furious."

I wonder what it's like to be a tadpole...

Meanwhile, the brooms were still dashing in and out, up and down the steps. And, all the time, the water was getting deeper.

I wish I could swim.

Soon it reached Max's knees... then his waist... then his chest.

SPLASH! SPLOSH! The brooms flung a few more pails of water into the room. Waves washed across the workshop.

Tabitha shot past, trying to surf.

Argh mmf
flaffle ploff!

"I warned you not to try any spells,"
she spluttered, spitting out water.
"Maybe next time you'll listen to me."

"If this goes on, there won't *be* a next time," muttered Max, desperately. "Help!" he yelled, climbing onto a table.

Somebody help!

But he knew there was no one around to hear.

Suddenly, there was a loud pop. Sticklewick appeared in a shower of green sparks.

341

Before he could
catch his breath,
the two brooms
flew down the steps
and flung yet more
water into the workshop.

"Galloping goblins!" cried the sorcerer. "What *has* that boy been doing?"

Quickly, he raised his wand and spoke the magic words.

Eye of bat and tooth of boar, return to how you were before!

In a flash, one of the brooms vanished. The other whizzed across the room and stood neatly against a table.

Finally, with a loud glug-glug-glug, the water began to drain away.

Nervously, Max climbed down from the table. His knees felt weak.

I'm in for it now.

Sticklewick glared at him. "Well? What have you got to say for yourself?"

"Um... I'm really sorry..."
"Not good enough!" roared Sticklewick.
"I warned you. Now it's tadpole time."

Max dived behind the water tank. "*Please* don't turn me into a tadpole," he cried. "I won't ever meddle with magic again."

"No, you won't," snapped Sticklewick.
"Tadpoles can't do simple spells and they
certainly can't do tricky ones..."

He paused and thought for a second.
Max didn't dare move.

Hmm... that was
quite a difficult
spell you did...

Just then, Tabitha spoke. "He might be a good sorcerer one day... Maybe you should start teaching him magic."

He is
your apprentice
after all...

"Maybe..." said Sticklewick, "but first he cleans up here." He turned to Max. "And if you *ever* disobey me again, you'll be frogspawn in the moat."

From that day on, Max was a perfect pupil. Soon he learned how to do spells properly. And when he grew up, he became a great sorcerer...

...although he was always a little afraid of broomsticks.

About the stories

King Donkey Ears

King Donkey Ears is based on an Irish folktale but that came from a much older legend about a king named Midas. King Midas was judging a competition between a musician and the god Apollo and declared the musician the winner. Apollo was so angry he gave King Midas donkey's ears.

The Enormous Turnip

The Enormous Turnip is a Russian folktale written by Count Alexei Tolstoy, who also wrote poems and novels.

The Inch Prince

The Inch Prince is based on a very old Japanese fairy tale called The One Inch Boy.

Androcles and the Lion

Androcles and the Lion is one of Aesop's Fables, a collection of short stories, first told in ancient Greece around 4,000 years ago. The stories are often about animals, and they always have a "moral" (a message or lesson) at the end.

Stone Soup

Stone Soup is based on an old folktale from Europe. In some countries, it is called Nail Soup and a nail is used instead of a stone.

The Sorcerer's Apprentice

The tale of the Sorcerer's Apprentice has been around for almost 2,000 years. The version here is based on a poem composed in 1797 by the German writer, Johann Wolfgang von Goethe.

Additional illustrations by Simona Dimitri